First published by Mijade Publications 2002.
This edition published 2003 by Macmillan Children's Books
a division of Macmillan Publishers Limited
20 New Wharf Road, London N1 9RR
Basingstoke and Oxford
Associated companies worldwide
www.panmacmillan.com

ISBN 0 333 98737 3 (HB)
ISBN 0 333 99287 3 (PB)

3 5 7 9 8 6 4 2 (PB)

A CIP catalogue record for this book is available
from the British Library.

Printed in Belgium.

Brigitte Minne

The Best Bottom

pictures by Marjolein Pottie

MACMILLAN CHILDREN'S BOOKS

Frog lived right in the middle of the farmyard. She was a kind and helpful frog and always said, " Good morning!" to the animals as they passed by her lilypad.

One day, she hopped into the farmyard
and found Peacock strutting about clucking noisily.
"Just look at my tail!" he was saying. "Did you ever see anything so graceful?
So bright and beautiful? And a beautiful tail makes a beautiful bottom.
That's what my mother always said."

"I've got a beautiful bottom, too," said Pig. "It's round and
pink as a lollipop. And I've got a little corkscrew tail.
I just don't go on about it."

When Donkey heard that he started braying. "Hah! Your bottom will come to a sticky end, my friend. What you need is a bottom like mine. Far more elegant, and much less tasty!"

"Elegant!" barked Dog. "A scrubby grey bottom with a flea-bitten tail?
My bottom is much smarter than yours."

The argument was all round the farmyard in no time. All the animals started looking at their bottoms and comparing them with everyone else's.

Cat and Horse, Rabbit and Goat,
Sheep and Cockerel, they all joined in.
But who really did have the best bottom?
Everyone wanted to know, even Frog.

The cows were the wisest, so they came up with a plan.
"How about holding a competition?" they said. "We cows could be the judges."

One of the cows wanted to enter the competition, but her sisters said she couldn't.
If a cow entered, and all the judges were cows, that wouldn't be fair. She'd be
bound to win.
    Everyone agreed, and all the other animals put their names forward.

Now it was time to get ready!
Rabbit pulled all the bits of grass out of her tail.
Dog combed his tail with his teeth and
chased away all the fleas.
Pig washed his bottom in the pond.
Everyone was busy.

Everyone except Frog. Poor Frog! She wanted to enter the competition, too, but she didn't think she stood a chance of winning. She was the only one who didn't have a tail. And what was a bottom without a tail?

"Never mind," she thought. "I'll enter anyway, just for fun."

Meanwhile, the other animals weren't having fun at all.
They were so desperate to win that they were all losing their temper.
Soon, everyone was squabbling.

Frog went to Cow and asked if she could enter the competition.
"Are you sure?" asked Cow. "But you haven't got a tail!
And what is a bottom without a tail?"
"It'll be fun," croaked Frog.
"All right, then," said Cow, and she put Frog's name down.

The other animals burst out laughing
when they heard Frog was entering.
"If I had a bottom like that, I'd stay at home,"
sniggered Donkey.

Frog smiled. She turned away and started
picking poppies and clover, daisies and dandelions.

"Look," said Pig. "Frog is making a bouquet for
the winner. Isn't that kind of her!"

At last the great day arrived.
The cow sisters sat at a long table and the other animals jostled
to get to the front. All except Frog, who hadn't arrived yet.

"First contestant step forward," called the cows.
"I'm first," shouted Peacock. "My bottom is best!"
"No it isn't!" barked Dog.
And that was that.
Everyone started pushing and shoving and
screaming at the tops of their voices.
"Mine is the best!"
"No, it isn't!"
"Yours is ugly!"
"Yours is silly!"
"At least mine's not pink!"
"Be quiet, Goat!"
"You be quiet, Cat!"

Then Goat aimed a good hard kick at Cat,
who dodged behind Rabbit.
"Ow!" cried Rabbit. He flew through the air …
and fell on Horse … who stepped on Cockerel …
who jumped on Donkey's back and started
pecking his ears.

Then everyone started fighting. Fur and feathers flew everywhere
and all those pampered bottoms got very tatty.

At that moment, Frog made her entrance.
"Wow!" gasped the cow sisters. "Nice tail!"
They clapped their hooves, and cried, "Frog is the winner!
Frog has the best bottom of all!"

"Well done Frog!" called all the animals. But they were really very ashamed of themselves, and they slunk off with their tails between their legs.

And Frog? She jumped for joy – all the way back to her pond!